A RAINFOREST ADVENTURE

JASPER - AMAZON PARROT BOOK 1

SHARON C. WILLIAMS

CHAPTER ONE

Trees grew so high that it was hard to tell where they ended and where the sky began. Trees with large, bright green leaves were covered with orchids, their branches reaching toward the sky. The forest buzzed with so much activity every single day. Today was no exception.

The jungle had many animals, some of which were the Amazon parrots. They wore all the colors of the rainbow. Their cheeks were a mixture of red, yellow, and orange feathers, while on their forehead was a beautiful explosion of violet. Their bodies were as green as the grass in your backyard, and their tail feathers completed the masterpiece with colors from black to blue to red. These birds seemed to know just how magnificent they were by the way they flew around showing off.

Normally, there was nothing extraordinary about a hollow tree in the middle of the rainforest, yet this one had something special. Halfway up was a hole covered with leaves and twigs. Inside, there was the nest belonging to an Amazon parrot.

However, if you looked ... really looked, you would see that eggs had been laid within that nest. Sally stood by, keeping her eggs warm. She watched and waited for that magical day. Inside the eggs, however, all was quiet and dark.

Soon, it was time for the eggs to hatch. Sally tapped on the eggs.

A curious tapping came from within one of them. As sunlight peeked through the leaves, the egg cracked down the middle. Slowly, the shell broke apart. A tiny beak appeared as the young one worked his way out.

Who?

Well ... Jasper, that's who. With his eyes closed and feather-less body shaking, he fell onto his face, looking quite pitiful.

From behind, he heard, "Hi, Jasper. I'm your mama. I've been waiting for you."

"Jasper? What's a Jasper?"

"That's you, silly," she said. "Pretty soon your brother or sister will hatch, too."

Suddenly, Jasper's stomach made a loud rumbling noise.

Knowing how hungry he must be, Sally fed him.

As his tummy got full, Jasper got sleepy and slowly fell asleep. It had been a busy morning for the little bird.

THE NEXT DAY, movement broke the silence within the nest just enough to wake up Jasper. He heard his mama coaching the other egg to crack.

She nudged and nudged, but the egg remained uncracked.

Jasper watched his mama continue to stare at the egg.

She sighed.

"What's wrong with it?" he asked his mama.

"I don't know, son. There could be a few reasons. Maybe I

didn't sit on it enough to keep it warm. Maybe it doesn't have a baby inside. I'm not sure," she said.

Jasper didn't know what to say to his mama. While he didn't know what it would be like to have a brother or sister, having one would have given him company for the times his mama was out gathering food and supplies. What he did know was that she was sad. Maybe that was what he was feeling on the inside of his tiny body.

Mama came to where Jasper sat and gave him a big hug. "It wasn't meant to be. A lesson we all learn as we grow older, Jasper."

At that moment, Jasper's tummy made a loud noise.

A smile found its way across his mama's face. She left to find food for her little man. Quickly returning, she fed him until he was satisfied.

Soon, Jasper fell asleep.

Waking up the next day, he was startled to find the most curious sight staring back at him with its eyes blinking.

"Who are you?" Jasper asked, keeping his distance from the ugly thing.

"I'm Willie, your brother," he said.

"But ... you weren't here when I went to bed. Where did you come from?"

"I hatched last night. Mama said I'm a late bloomer. I think that means I'm special," Willie said.

The two young birds watched each other for a long time, each thinking how ugly the other was.

Secretly, Jasper thought he was prettier, but he kept that to himself. He wanted his feathers to start growing so that he could look like a real bird, just like his mama.

Who cares if I had a brother!?

"This is so cool," Willie said. "Did she tell you what we are?"

"Yes, we are Yellow Cheek Amazons," Jasper replied proudly.

It was a mouthful to say, and while he was still new to all of this, such a title had to mean something awesome. He just knew it. There was so much to learn. Jasper felt that he was ready. Best of all, he now had someone to do things with.

He looked outside of his nest and noticed how high up in the tall trees they were. So high, that it hurt his neck. So many unfamiliar sounds also filled the air. He was amazed.

For the next two weeks, the routine stayed the same. Day in and day out, the little birds ate, pooped, and slept. The changes were slight. Both boys' feathers were growing like tiny spikes poking out of a pin cushion.

They were also growing a little bit with each passing day. Like most boys, they were also getting restless.

Waking up one day to a loud sound, Jasper's eyes opened wide. Seeing Willie by the entrance, he asked, "What's going on, Willie? You woke me up from a good sleep with the ruckus you're making."

"Sorry, but this is so awesome, I could not hold back. You can sleep any time, Jasper," his brother said. "Come check this out."

Jasper walked over to the entrance of their nest and stood by his brother's side. Looking in the direction Willie was staring at, he saw a large group of birds flying across the horizon.

"Wow. That looks like so much fun. I can't wait until our wings are fully grown."

"Why wait?" Willie asked.

"Well, duh. We would fall," Jasper said, thinking to himself that Willie must have hit his head while sleeping to come up with such a suggestion.

"No, we won't," Willie replied, flapping his tiny wings. "All we have to do is the same as those guys and don't stop."

"Mama said it would be a few more weeks before we could start to fly," Jasper reminded his brother.

"What, you're chicken?" Willie goaded. A smile formed upon his face.

Now, if anyone knows anything about anything, they know that no one likes to be called chicken, especially by their baby brother.

"Mama just left before you woke up. She will be gone for a bit," Willie continued.

Willie apparently had forgotten it was due to him that Jasper had been woken up from a good sleep.

Not wanting to be the one to back down, Jasper said, "Okay. Let's do it. You're right. How hard can this be?"

"I saw the birds just lift off, so if we jumped out that should do the trick," Willie suggested.

Both brothers looked at each other for a few minutes and then looked back out. In unison, they jumped out of the nest, flapping their tiny wings. Instead of flying with ease like they'd seen the other birds do, they started to fall, and fast.

"Flap, Jasper, flap!" Willie yelled as he did the same.

"It's not working!" Jasper shot back.

Both of them continued to fall toward the ground. It didn't take long for the two of them to hit the soft leaves lining the floor of the jungle.

Looking around, Jasper searched for his brother, but he was nowhere in sight. "Willie ... Willie? Where are you?" Jasper shouted.

Nothing.

"Willie ... Willieee?" he repeated.

Again, nothing.

Jasper shivered. It was a bit cooler down here than it was up in their nest.

Where could Willie be? he wondered. *Okay, don't worry. How far could he be?*

Jasper looked up and saw how far he'd fallen. This wasn't good. He should have never listened to Willie. The leaves rustled from the small breeze making its way to the bottom. It reminded Jasper of where he was.

Should he sit here and wait, or start looking for Willie? He honestly didn't know what to do. He would call out for Willie one more time, and then move on. Sitting here wasn't going to help either of them at all.

"Willie? Willie? Come on, stop playing, Willie!" Jasper yelled.

Jasper took a deep breath and walked slowly from where he'd landed, taking the time to cry out Willie's name, just in case. Taking small steps, Jasper arched his head and kept a lookout for his brother. He had to find him. He didn't want to be all alone in this strange place.

When he'd thought Willie hadn't made it, Jasper mourned him, not truly understanding what it meant to have a brother. What he knew now was that he didn't want to be by himself. He wanted his brother with him; someone who was just like him, who understood what it was like to be a young parrot.

Jasper made his way to the nearest tree and rested near it for a tiny bit. He was scared, hungry, and now alone. He also had no way of getting back home. Although afraid to close his eyes, his eyelids closed from exhaustion because of the failed attempt at flying.

He didn't know how long they were closed when the sound of movement stirred him awake. Looking straight ahead, he saw a brown blob coming straight toward him. Well, it was half blob and half leaves. He leaned back against the tree as much as possible. Jasper gulped, trying to be brave.

The blob drew closer, the leaves falling off by the second. With each step it took, the shape became clearer to Jasper. The blob was not a blob. It was Willie!

Jasper ran. He met his brother halfway, hugging him tight. Some of the mud and remaining leaves were transferred onto him.

Chuckling, Willie said, "Good to see you again, too, Jasper."

He stepped back to give Willie a chance to breathe. Jasper asked," What happened to you? You were nowhere near me when I landed."

"I landed in some mud and as I got out, the leaves just stuck to me. I called out your name, but you never answered."

"I did the same thing, calling out your name three times."

"I heard you call my name and started walking toward where I thought I heard it. We didn't fall that far from each other, but the mud slowed me down."

Hugging his brother again, Jasper said, "I'm glad you found me. It wasn't fun being out here alone. This is a very scary place."

"Yes, it is." Willie tried to pick the remaining leaves off himself. He then looked up. "Hey, have you thought about how we're going to get back home before Mama gets back?"

Jasper paused and thought about it. No, he hadn't. He'd been too busy being worried about finding Willie to think of anything else.

"Oh, boy. No, I haven't. What are we going to do now? This is all your fault, Willie!"

"I didn't make you jump! Well, not really," Willie said.

Jasper looked at his brother. Fighting wasn't going to solve their problem.

"Well, we can't fly back up, and we can't stay here either. Maybe Mama is already back at home."

Willie shuddered. "She is going to be mad."

"She will be worried, too," Jasper said.

"Yeah, but she'll mostly be mad."

Jasper lapsed into silence. Willie was right. There had to be a way to figure this out. While he pondered their predicament, a small stick fell nearby.

Looking up, Jasper noticed a yellow bird flying toward them. "Hello," he said to the bird.

"Hello," the bird replied. "You two aren't, by chance, the two birds that fell out of the nest earlier, are you?"

"We didn't fall," Willie spoke up. "We were flying."

Even Jasper knew how silly that sounded.

Hiding a grin, the bird replied, "Call it what you like. All I know is I saw you fall like two little rocks. I've been trying to find you. I'm sure your mom is very worried about you both."

"Do you know where we live?" Jasper asked.

"Sure do. Way up there," the bird stated, and pointed upward.

"Could you go tell our mama where we are?"

"Yes, please. Can you help us out?" Willie chimed in.

"Sure. My name is Al, by the way. What are your names?"

"I am Jasper, and this is my brother, Willie."

"Nice to meet you. Okay, let me go see if I can find your mom at your nest."

With a salute of his wings, Al jumped up and flew upward, higher and higher until the two birds could no longer see him.

"We might as well sit here and wait," Jasper said.

Sighing, Willie replied, "How mad do you think Mama will be?"

"I'm not sure, but what's worse, having Mama mad at us, or spending the night here?"

Both boys knew they wouldn't survive a night on the jungle floor alone. They didn't have their complete feathers and it did get cold at night. Fortunately, the two didn't have to wait long, for they soon heard their mama calling out their names.

WITHIN A FEW MINUTES, Sally appeared from above and softly landed next to her two boys. Opening her wings, the two ran to hug her. She held them tightly to her body.

"Mama, I can't breathe! You're hugging us too tightly!" Willie complained.

"You are lucky that's your only problem, young man!" she replied, releasing them so that she could get a good look at them. She wanted to make sure they were okay.

"Do you two know how worried I was? Coming home to feed you and seeing the nest empty?"

"Yes, Mama," the two young parrots mumbled.

Ignoring their response, Sally continued, "Then, I find out from the birds nearby that you jumped out of the nest and fell to the ground."

"We saw the other birds flying. We thought we could do it, too," Willie said in a small voice.

She looked at Jasper. "Do you have anything to say for yourself?"

"Sorry, Mama," he said, staring at the ground.

"Just promise me you won't do this again until I tell you that you're ready. This goes for the both of you."

Sally stared at her two pitiful boys.

Jasper was still staring at the ground, while Willie was covered in mud and leaves.

"Okay, let's get you both back home. Jasper, wait here while I take Willie home first. I'll be right back."

With that, she gently grabbed Willie by the neck and took off.

———————

WHY DID she take Willie first? He was the one who made me jump in the first place. This isn't fair! he thought irritably. Jasper stomped his feet into the leaves. *He's probably getting all cleaned up while I'm sitting here waiting.*

The time went by slowly, or so Jasper thought. In all actuality, only a few short minutes had passed before Mama reappeared to return Jasper to the nest. When they got back, Jasper saw that Willie had started to clean himself up.

Mama only made it worse by walking over to him to help pick off some of the remaining leaves.

Really?

Jasper made his way toward the opposite side of the nest, making sure he made as much noise as possible.

Looking up, Mama asked, "What's wrong, Jasper?"

"Nothing."

Seeing that he wasn't going to say anymore, Mama made her way over to where he sat.

"What's wrong, Jasper?" she asked again.

"Why did you pick up Willie first?"

"Well, he had mud and leaves on him. I needed to get him started on getting clean before it completely dried up."

"He started it. He made me jump out!"

"He made you?" Mama said, and smiled.

"Okay. He didn't MAKE me, but you still picked him up first. You love him more."

"No, Jasper," she said softly. "I love you both equally. Willie is the youngest and he needs more care. Now, if that had been you at the opening of the nest, would you have thought to jump out?"

"No."

"Why not?"

"I know my wings weren't ready."

"See, you know this, while Willie isn't as grown up as you. Jasper, it's your job as a big brother to make sure he is okay and to also look after him."

"Really?"

"Yes, and I'm depending on you to help me when I'm not here. Okay?"

Jasper nodded, relieved. "Yes, Mama."

"And Jasper? I love you," Mama said, hugging him to her. "How about you go help your brother out? He's a mess, isn't he?"

Giggling, Jasper nodded and made his way over to where Willie was and helped him clean up.

Between the two of them, the job was completed in no time.

Once fed, Jasper, Willie, and his mother soon took a nap to rest up from the day's adventure.

CHAPTER TWO

Morning arrived too soon. With the two boys exhausted from their previous exploits, the night came and went by very fast. Waking up, they saw Mama watching over them.

Looking at himself and then at Willie, Jasper said, "What's wrong?"

"Nothing," Mama replied, "I just like looking at my boys. Especially with that scare we had yesterday."

From behind Jasper, Willie's stomach growled and it wouldn't stop.

"Guess it's time to go get food for all of us. Now, boys, I expect to see you both in this nest when I get back, right?"

"Yes, Mama," Jasper and Willie said in unison.

"Good. And while I'm gone, Jasper will be in charge."

"Oh, man!" Willie cried, wrapping his wings around his body and pouting.

Jasper puffed his chest out just a tad. He was in charge and liked the sound of that.

"That's right, Willie. You have to do what I say. Right, Mama?"

"Jasper, you have to be fair now. I'm putting you in charge because I trust you to take care of your baby brother."

"He's only older by one day," Willie muttered irritably.

"Willie ..." Mama sighed.

"Yes, Mama, I'll behave," Willie replied, walking toward the back of the nest and sitting down.

"I won't be too long. Just enough to get food to feed those hungry bellies," Mama said.

With that, she hurried to the tree's entrance and took off in search of food.

I'm in charge. I'm in charge. I'm in charge. Woohoo!

Granted, there was only so much they could do in the nest. In fact, there was really only one thing for Jasper to do—to make sure Willie didn't do anything stupid that would get the both of them in trouble. Or worse, hurt. It would be a piece of cake. After the scare, Jasper doubted Willie was up for that to happen again. It could get boring, but that was a-okay for him.

Turning around, he walked over to where Willie sat. "So what should we do?" Jasper asked.

"Nothing fun, that's for sure."

"We could groom the feathers we have, or we can look outside. Maybe we can play pretend?"

"Boring, boring, and boring," was Willie's reply.

Jasper shook his little head. Being in charge was turning out to not be as fun as he'd first thought. Seeing how Willie refused to be in a good mood, Jasper walked toward the entrance so that the morning light that managed to filter through the trees would shine on him. He so loved the warmth. He liked how it enveloped him as the dust bunnies filtered through the air.

Jasper closed his eyes and daydreamed about flying. His mama had told him and Willie it would be soon. It would only be a matter of time before they would be out there flying in the sky with their mama and learning more about their jungle home. Jasper was so caught up in the excitement that he'd stopped paying attention to his surroundings.

Minutes flew by as his daydream came to a close. Jasper opened his eyes.

Ah, life was good!

"Hey, Willie, come on. Let's do something," he said, turning around. "Willie?"

Willie was looking right at Jasper, but he didn't reply.

"Oh, come on! I know you're mad at Mama for putting me in charge, but we can still have fun," Jasper replied as a matter-of-factly.

Willie didn't speak, nor did he blink. Willie lowered his eyes and stared at his wing before looking back up at Jasper. He did this three times.

What was going on? Was this a new game? Jasper thought, moving closer to Willie.

"What's wrong? Are you okay?"

That was when Jasper saw them. They were red, had a lot of legs, and they were also small. Red ants!

Jasper froze. Mama had told them stories of the ants that crawled upon the floor of the jungle. How anything that got in their way was either killed or destroyed. They had powerful jaws that wouldn't just bite, but inject their venom into their victims. Mama had said more, but Jasper couldn't remember what it was. His eyes were glued to the ants that were crawling all over his brother.

Jasper was in charge and it was up to him to help Willie out. That's what big brothers do, his mother had told him. He was so busy trying to figure out what to do that he failed to notice the red ants were now crawling onto his feet.

He felt his heart drop to the bottom of his chest. His mouth went dry as he looked at his brother.

Willie remained frozen.

Neither boy could afford to move for fear of being bitten.

Great! My first chance at being in charge and this has to happen!

Jasper knew he couldn't panic and he couldn't move, but that was all he knew.

"What do we do?" Willie whispered.

"I don't know," Jasper replied.

Both continued to stand as still as possible.

The ants continued to crawl upon them, making their way up their bodies toward their beaks.

Jasper's eyes were glued on the ants moving across his brother, while he felt the ants crawl over him. He wanted to cry, but if he did that, he knew it would scare Willie. He had to be strong for his brother's sake, no matter what. His mama was depending on him.

"Willie, close your eyes and just hold still. They will move on if we don't bother them," Jasper whispered.

Jasper had no clue if they would move on, but he hoped they would. Seeing that Willie had closed his eyes, Jasper did the same.

The ants continued to crawl about, checking out the birds from claw to beak.

Come on, leave!

Jasper refused to panic. He would not let his mama down, but he was starting to get scared. Opening his eyes slowly, he took a peek at Willie to find that his eyes were still closed. He wondered what Willie was thinking. Hearing movement outside, Jasper hoped it meant that their mama was arriving with food, but more importantly, to help.

"Jasper! Willie!" Mama cried with alarm. "Don't move!"

Horror filled her as she saw the situation that was occurring inside of her home.

Jasper had no intention of moving. He was pretty sure that

Willie felt the same way. He felt Mama pick the ants off of his beak one by one. He also saw her do the same for Willie, tossing the pesky ants out through the nest's hole. Jasper soon sighed with relief. It was safe again.

"Yeah! You killed them!" Before Willie could get any further, his mother interrupted him.

"No, Willie, I didn't kill them. I tossed them out so that they'd find their way home."

"But ... they were on my beak!" he exclaimed.

"They were just doing what ants do. How can we blame them for that?"

"I can blame them," he muttered to no one in particular.

"Are you two okay?" she asked, looking at the two of them.

"Yes, Mama, but I was scared that they were going to bite me," Jasper chimed in.

"I was scared even more," Willie said, trying to one up Jasper.

"It doesn't matter who was more scared, so long as you are both okay. How did you know to stay so still?"

"I didn't. Jasper told me what to do."

Mama smiled. "I'm very proud of you, Jasper. You were very brave."

Jasper didn't feel very brave. The only reason he'd stood still was because he was scared, too. Anyone would have done the same thing. He didn't have time to think more on it.

Willie was already lining up to be fed. If Jasper didn't hurry, Willie would pig out.

Once he and Willie were fed, it was time for them to groom their still growing feathers.

Mama did the same. The only difference was that she had so many more to clean.

Once the tedious task was done, the three of them settled in for a nap.

While Willie and their mother fell asleep rather quickly, Jasper could not. He had a lot on his mind. His mother had told him he was brave, but he really didn't do anything. She'd placed him in charge of Willie, but what about the dangers that Jasper wouldn't be able to fix?

This was a huge responsibility he'd been given. What happened when they finally learned how to fly? There was so much out there that Jasper had to learn. The unknown worried him. He didn't have the same faith that his mama had in him.

Jasper sighed. He cuddled up next to Willie, who was sound asleep. Yawning, Jasper closed his eyes. He would worry about everything later.

CHAPTER THREE

Today was THE DAY. Today, Jasper and his brother would learn how to fly.

YIPPEE!

Jasper tapped his brother awake. "Wake up. Wake up. It's time, Willie. It's time!"

A few days ago, their mama had told them that since they were fully fledged they could start practicing their flying. Fledging was just a fancy way to say that all of their feathers had grown out and that they were growing up.

Willie peeked out of the tree, saw how far down it was, and gulped. It was far. Really, really far.

"We're ready, Mama," Jasper said, not even waiting for Willie.

"Are you sure?" she asked with a smile.

He and Willie nodded, making their way toward the nest's opening.

Oh, boy!

Before either boy could change his mind, Mama tossed

them out into the air. The two of them free-fell toward the ground.

From above, they both heard, "Flap your wings fast."

Jasper stretched his tiny wings out and flapped them for dear life.

Willie did the same.

No matter how hard they tried, they were still heading straight for the ground.

Here we go again, Jasper thought.

The young birds panicked. They closed their eyes and plopped on the floor of the jungle. The leaves and underbrush broke their fall, so neither of them were hurt.

PHEW!

The sounds and smells were different from what they were used to within the tree, but there was also a slight familiarity to it from the previous fall.

I can't see the sky from here, Jasper thought.

Without any warning, a brown creature with a long tail and long arms appeared.

Willie ran behind Jasper and peeked around him with only his face showing.

"What is that?" he asked.

"How am I supposed to know?"

Jasper was so surprised that he wanted to ask who the creature was. Instead, when he opened his mouth, the only thing that came out was, "What are you?"

The creature laughed. "I'm a spider monkey, and my name is Charlie." Charlie drew closer to them and held out his hands for a handshake. "Who are you?" he asked.

"My name is Jasper, and this is my brother, Willie. We are Amazon parrots and we live high above in the trees."

"You came from way up there?" Charlie wondered, and looked up. "Wow. I've never had anyone drop in on me before from that high up. Awesome! So, what are you doing down here if you're from all the way up there?"

"We're learning to fly. Today was our first try," Jasper said.

He didn't want to mention the first failed attempt. He was too embarrassed.

Charlie chuckled. "You might want to try again."

That's when it hit Jasper. *How are we supposed to get back up to the nest? This needing to be saved thing is getting old. Don't panic. Mama knows where we are, I hope.*

From above, they all heard a ruffle as their mama flew down beside them.

Gently, she picked Willie up and flew high into the sky. Before Jasper had a chance to complain, she returned and scooped him up, flying higher and higher to get back home.

Jasper knew better than to complain about not being picked up first. *But it would be nice if she picked me up before Willie.*

Once they were back home, Mama asked if they wanted to try again.

Both of them declined.

"You're sure? Practice, practice, and more practice is the best way to learn," she said.

"I landed on my butt. Do you know how much that hurts?" Willie fussed, rubbing his butt.

Jasper laughed at that. Poor, Willie. If something like that bothered him, he needed all the help he could get from him and his mama. It was going to take time for him and his brother to learn how to fly.

He and Willie settled in to take their nap. There would be plenty of time for flying later.

CHAPTER FOUR

"Ready?"

Both boys woke up to the sound of their mama's voice.

Slowly, Jasper opened his eyes and again without warning, he was tossed out of the tree.

Flap, flap, flap. That's right, I need to flap my wings, Jasper thought.

Once again, the ground drew closer by the second. He flapped faster and closed his eyes, ready to fall yet again to the ground.

Here I go again!

However, instead of falling, Jasper rose higher and higher.

Wait a minute, he thought, feeling the wind beneath him. *I'm flying!*

Sure enough, he was. The sky had never looked as grand as it did right now.

"Ahhhhhhhhhhhhhhhhhhhhhhhhhhhhhhhhhh."

What was that noise?

Before he could think about it much longer, Willie dropped past him.

Jasper hoped he would be lucky as well.

"Wheeeeeeeeeeeeeeeeeeeeeeeeeeeeee!"

Willie flew up beside Jasper with a look of joy upon his face.

From behind, their mama flew up next to them.

The three of them flew high above the treetops of the rainforest, enjoying the moment. The successful flight was short as the trio returned to their nest.

As they arrived back at the hollow tree, Jasper thought about what a great morning it had been.

"Oh, boy. Oh, boy," Willie gushed. "When can we try again, Mama? When?"

Chuckling, Mama said, "Soon, son, soon. Jasper, did you enjoy it also?"

"Yes, that was so much fun. It sure beats falling."

The three of them burst into laughter.

Flying was tiring, but fun. No longer would he and Willie be stuck in the nest. There would be chances for exploring later, but right now, it was time to nap.

As sleep overcame him, he thought, *Wait until I show Charlie I can fly!*

It had been a few weeks since the trio last saw each other. The last time their friend had seen the two of them was on the bottom of the jungle floor.

CHAPTER FIVE

As Jasper woke up to a new day, he thought something seemed different. Everything around him was a tad smaller. Even inside the nest, the space seemed to have dwindled. He was able to see a bit further out from the tree. Jasper stretched his wings, but there wasn't enough room.

Turning to the left, he saw that Willie was still asleep. *I'll let him sleep. I'll fly on down to the river.* He was curious about what it was like there. *Mama talked about it all the time.*

As he got ready to take off, he heard, "Where are you going?"

Darn, Willie woke up!

"I was going to explore a bit. You were asleep, and I didn't want to bother you."

"You were going to leave me?" Willie asked in disbelief.

"No, not really," Jasper said, even though that was exactly what he'd planned.

"Where's Mama?" Willie asked.

"She went to visit some friends for a small while."

"Did she say we could leave?"

"Yes, so long as we tell someone where we are going," Jasper replied.

"Cool, let's go," Willie replied, moving to where Jasper was standing.

Sighing, Jasper took off with Willie in tow. The two of them flew to the nearest tree, sitting on a branch closest to the nest.

Their neighbor, Mrs. Peabody, sat at the entrance looking out.

"Hello, Mrs. Peabody," Jasper said.

"Hello, Jasper. Hello, Willie," she replied.

"Hello, Mrs. Peabody," Willie said. "What are you staring at?"

"Oh, nothing in particular. I just enjoy looking at the sky. It's so pretty with its different shades of blue."

"Ma'am, Mama said we could go out and play if we told you where we were going," Jasper said.

"Oh, yes, she did mention that before she left. Where are the two of you headed?"

"Down to the river to see if we can find our friend, Charlie," Jasper said.

"I will tell her when I see her. Be careful," said Mrs. Peabody.

"Thank you, ma'am," the boys replied in unison before flying away.

The pair neared the river's edge, flying down to take a peek. As the boys landed, they saw Charlie and waved to him.

Oh, boy, here's my chance to show him my new wings, thought Jasper.

"Hi, Jasper. Hi, Willie. I see you got your wings. Congratulations! Pretty cool. It's been a while since I've seen the two of you," Charlie said.

"Thank you," the boys replied in unison.

They walked toward the edge of the water. Leaning forward to get a drink, Jasper suddenly jumped back.

Willie jumped back also, not knowing why Jasper had done so in the first place.

"What's wrong?" Charlie prodded.

"I saw something staring back at me!" Jasper cried.

"It's you, silly! It's your reflection in the water."

"It can't be me. It's soooooooooooooooo big." Jasper looked around, afraid.

"Jasper, you're growing up fast, if I do say so myself. You both are," Charlie pointed out.

Jasper leaned over for another peek and saw something staring back at him again.

Willie did the same. This time, they both knew it was their reflections staring back at them.

Amazing!

Their feathers were so full and colorful. The boys had seen their mama's feathers, but had never truly paid attention to their own in such detail before. Bright colored feathers covered Jasper and Willie.

Their nape was red. Jasper and Willie's tail feathers were outlined in black and blue, while their cheeks were yellow and orange. A spot of purple feathers also graced both of their heads. Wow, they looked just like their mama!

"I'm all grown up!" Jasper proudly announced.

"Me too, me too!" Willie piped in.

"Not so fast, you two. You have a long way to go before you're done growing. The forest is big and full of different creatures, plants, and sounds. There are a lot of things to do and explore. As you explore, what you learn will shape you into who you will be when you are fully grown," Charlie said.

"You know so much, Charlie. How old are you?" Willie asked.

"Oh, I've been around a few years. I've learned when to play and when to work. When to hide and when to sleep. When to eat and when to rest. You will learn these things, too, in time. There are many dangers in the jungle. One lesson that you must never forget is to listen to your mother. She knows what is best for you and will teach you all you need to know. She will prepare you for the time when you leave the nest. Until then, watch, listen, and learn."

Jasper felt warm inside. He had a family and Charlie, who loved him and would be there to help him when he needed it. This was a special day, indeed.

CHAPTER SIX

The days passed quickly. Jasper's feathers were healthy and gorgeous. So were Willie's. The two of them were getting pretty good at grooming them, which was a necessity. Preening was a way for a bird to keep its feathers clean and neat. Now that the two of them were fully fledged, this was a full-time job.

One afternoon, Willie decided to go visit Charlie. "Hey, Jasper, how about we go see what Charlie is up to?"

It had been a while since the duo had visited their friend. Getting permission from their mama, they flew down toward the bottom of the tree that housed their nest. Not that far from the base of their tree, Charlie was soon spotted swinging from a tree nearby using his tail.

"Hi, Charlie. What are you up to today?" Jasper asked.

"I'm waiting for my friend, George, so we can go for a walk," the monkey said. "You can come with us, if you like."

"Is George a monkey like you?" Willie inquired.

"Oh, no, he is nothing like me at all. Just wait and you will see."

The boys nodded.

This should be fun, meeting someone new, Jasper thought.

As they waited, they talked about the things that had happened since they last saw each other.

Charlie looked up and stared at something behind Willie. "Here he comes."

An interesting animal soon came into sight. Jasper thought his brother was ugly when he'd first seen him, but what he saw before him was even uglier.

I'm going to have to apologize to Willie for thinking he was ugly, he thought.

What he saw before him was a creature that looked about the same size as Charlie. He was brown, but had a short tail. Each foot had three claws.

What an unusual animal. He was also walking so slow.

Be nice, Jasper. This is Charlie's friend.

"Hi, Charlie. Who are your friends?" the creature asked.

"Jasper, Willie, this is George. He's a sloth. George, these are my friends, Jasper and Willie. They are Amazon parrots."

"Nice to meet you two," George said.

"Likewise, George," Jasper replied.

"Likewise, George," Willie said, copying Jasper.

"Where do you live?" George questioned.

"They live all the way up there," Charlie answered for them, pointing to the sky.

"Wow!" George said.

Everyone laughed at his reaction. The group moved forward as they began their journey.

A few minutes later, George said, "Hey, slow down. I can't walk that fast."

Looking for answers, the two birds looked at Charlie.

"Remember, I said George is a sloth?"

Willie and Jasper nodded.

"They are slow moving animals. We can't walk too fast, or

George will be left behind. Sorry, George, I forgot to mention this to Jasper and Willie."

"That's okay. So long as they know not to walk too fast, I will be okay."

Jasper, Willie, and Charlie all agreed to take their time so that everyone would have a good time together.

The jungle floor fascinated Jasper. He'd met Charlie and now George. It was also here that he and Willie had fallen a few times. The first time had taught him the lesson his mama had tried to teach him, that he was to watch over his brother, Willie.

The view was incredible and so different from the nest up high. Along the way were leaves, leaves, and more leaves. There was very little light shining through from above. All around him he heard crackling sounds.

Looking at George and Charlie, Jasper asked, "What is that loud sound?"

Charlie's eyes widened. "That's the sound of red army ants, and from the sounds of it, it's a BIG army."

"They sound really, really close, Charlie," Willie said in a small voice.

"Be careful," George replied.

Willie looked at Jasper.

Jasper could only imagine that he was reliving the first time they'd met the ants. He walked over to where Willie was, just in case his brother needed help, and not just because it was his job to keep his brother safe. He was worried also.

"There they are," Charlie said, pointing to a spot in front of the group.

An army of ants was going up and down a tree. Leaves were being transported to somewhere in the distance.

Turning his head, Jasper saw Willie had completely stopped within his tracks. His eyes were glued to the ants.

"They won't bother you if you leave them alone," Charlie said aloud to any who would listen.

I bet he never had ants on him before, Jasper thought.

Making sure there were no ants behind them, Jasper said, "Willie, it's okay. Just back up slowly. I am here with you."

His brother slowly nodded, doing as Jasper asked of him.

Charlie and George liked the idea as well. They, too, were walking slowly backwards. Once they'd gotten a good distance away, the band of friends stopped.

Before Jasper could say a word, Willie came up and hugged him.

"I'm so glad you were here with me, Jasper. Ants still scare me, but it was nice to not be alone," he said.

Jasper had been scared as well, but he didn't have time to panic.

"I agree," George replied. "It was sure nice to not be alone with the ants. If it had just been me, I would have frozen up."

"Thank goodness for friends," Charlie piped in.

Everyone sighed with relief.

Looking up, George saw how fast the night was approaching. "It's getting late, everyone. Maybe we should all head home," he suggested.

Between the army ants and the darkening sky, everyone agreed they should head back home. Any minute now, a storm could break wide open. It was the nature of the Amazon. The walk would be shortened, but the gang didn't want to get caught in the rain or be the ants' next meal.

CHAPTER SEVEN

The sound of thunder broke through the air, making the forest take notice. The sky opened up and let loose on all the life below, pouring rain down upon the forest floor.

Guess I'm stuck inside the nest in this tree, Jasper thought.

Looking over to where Willie slept, it was comforting to know he wasn't alone. Jasper was happy that Willie had hatched after all. It would have been very quiet and different if that hadn't happened.

Jasper groomed himself while thinking about the day ahead of him. Taking care of one's feathers was a tedious job that took so long. He was exhausted by the time he was done. The rain was still pouring and it didn't seem like it was ever going to stop. It could rain for days on end in the jungle. Mama had told him so.

Before Jasper could plan his next move, a flash of lightning lit the sky. He looked out of the nest and studied his surroundings closely. A Toucan with a black body and yellow face, whose beak was long and painted with the shades of a rainbow, passed into his view. Large and dark green leaves were everywhere. It didn't seem to care about the weather.

He could also see a variety of colorful blooms from pink, white, orange, yellow, and even purple. There were fruit trees carrying the bright red and yellow of the mango, to the green and orange color of the papaya. The rainforest was a beautiful place to be, so full of life and so many different colors.

The clouds in the sky were full, dark, and wondrous to look at. He could make out the shape of a tree and not so far away was a cloud in the shape of a flower.

Hmm, I can keep myself company, he thought. *It's not so hard to do.*

He had to admit that things were much more fun with his brother around.

While the sky was amazing to look at, it also carried thunder clouds. Thunder scared Jasper. It was so loud that he jumped whenever it came without warning. He hated the noise and tended to huddle in the back of the nest, silently wishing that the rain would stop. He was anxious to go out and play.

How Willie and his mama did not wake up because of the thunder confused Jasper. Every time it thundered, it always disturbed his sleep. Willie and Mama were hard sleepers, she had told him. Jasper wished that was the case with him.

"Rain, rain, go away. Come on back another day."

Jasper sang the small tune his mama had taught him and Willie. He felt restless and wanted to explore again.

Suddenly, the storm stopped. The clouds broke open, and the sun shone through.

Jasper ruffled his feathers and shook off the rain drops that had fallen on him through the opening in the tree. The rain had felt good, and he liked being clean, even if it meant that it had to rain and thunder in order for him to take a bath.

Peeking out of the tree, he looked down, wondering about

the muddy ground below. It would be a shame to dirty himself now that he was clean. Besides, he was sleepy and a nap sounded just right. If Willie and his mother were to wake up and find Jasper missing, he knew they would worry and his mother would get upset. He didn't want to upset his family. Yeah, a nap sounded just about right.

CHAPTER EIGHT

Loud noises from outside the tree woke Jasper from his nap.

What was all the fuss? Did not everyone know he was trying to take a nap? How rude!

Jasper slowly stretched his body and walked over to the entrance of the tree. Before he could figure out what was going on, he saw something fly past him. A few seconds later, another blur flew by.

What in the world?

"Willie, come over here," Jasper said to his brother, who was now stretching himself awake.

Coming over to where Jasper was standing, Willie looked outside.

Jasper opened his eyes wide. He looked downward to see dozens of small bodies free-falling toward the floor of the jungle.

"Should we go see what's going on?" Willie asked.

"Yeah, let's do it," Jasper replied.

"Hold up, Jasper and Willie. I am coming with you," said Mama.

The boys waited while their mama got ready. Soon, the family flew out to see what was going on.

There was strength in numbers, Mama told them often enough. As Jasper flew down, the wind felt so good and cool against his feathers. He never tired of this feeling. Looking at his brother, Jasper saw a wide grin on his face.

I guess Willie feels the same way!

Their mama was close by, watching the action as well with a big smile on her face.

Flying was so much fun and it made Jasper feel so grown up. As he got closer to the commotion, he stretched out his feet to land on a tree branch nearby. On the jungle floor below him were a lot of baby parrots. Jasper cocked his head to the side and realized that it was their turn to learn how to fly. He never thought he would ever see so many trying at the same time.

"Do you boys want to stay and have fun?" Mama asked.

Jasper and Willie nodded.

The mama bird knew her boys were growing up and needed time outside of the nest.

"Don't stay out too long now."

Willie and Jasper agreed, watching Mama fly back up.

"I wonder if we looked that silly when we first fell?" Willie asked.

"And the second time," Jasper said.

The both of them laughed.

One by one, the babies were lifted back up to try again. Jasper was so glad that part was over for him. Landing that first time had certainly not been fun. As the jungle floor cleared, Jasper called out to Charlie, hoping his friend was around.

On cue, Charlie swung into view with some nuts in one hand.

Jasper wished he had a tail like Charlie, so he, too, would be able to swing from tree to tree. It seemed like a lot of fun.

"Hey, Jasper. Hey, Willie. What's up?" Charlie asked.

"I was just thinking how cool it would be to have a tail just like yours," he said.

Willie fanned his tail. He looked at Charlie's tail, and then at his own.

"Jasper's right. You can do so many things with it. Imagine, we could swing from tree to tree if we had one, Jasper."

"We would look rather silly, but that would be fun," he replied.

"It is pretty sweet, isn't it?" Charlie said, smiling.

The two parrots agreed.

"Want to explore some?" Jasper asked.

"Sure," Charlie replied, swooping down next to the pair. "Want to go see some new creatures?"

"New creatures? What kind?" the boys said in unison.

"Well, they are like you and me. They have two feet. They love fruit and nuts, and they are just at the edge of the jungle."

"Let's go," Jasper said, walking alongside Charlie.

Willie soon caught up.

The ground was still muddy, so Jasper flew to the nearest branch. Seeing Willie going through the mud, Jasper stopped him.

"Willie, you will make a mess in the nest if you keep tramping through the mud. Come on up to the branches."

As Willie did so, Charlie hopped onto a tree trunk.

Letting Charlie take the lead, the friends flew and swung from tree to tree. Eventually, the jungle thinned out as they got closer to the border.

Jasper and Willie had never been this far away from home. He was glad he wasn't alone. While he had to be brave for Willie's sake, it was nice to have his own security blanket— Charlie, who stood right next to him.

"Hey, Jasper, wanna hear a song I wrote about you?"

"You wrote a song about me?"

"Yup, I sure did. You too, Willie. All you have to do is replace Jasper's name in the song with Willie. It works for both names." Charlie cleared his throat. "Jasper, Jasper is my two-legged friend. He's the birdie in the green suit. He laughs with me. He sings with me. He's my Jasper. One more time!" Charlie sang. "Come on, sing with me."

Together, the three of them sang the song.

"Jasper, Jasper is my two-legged friend. He's the birdie in the green suit. He laughs with me. He sings with me. He's my Jasper."

Jasper laughed so hard that his sides hurt.

"Oh, wow, Charlie, that's awesome! And you are right, my name would fit in there nicely," Willie said.

"Charlie, that's so funny! I love that song. Thank you."

"You're welcome," Charlie replied.

"Why did you write a song about us anyway?" Willie asks.

Charlie shrugged. "You're both my friends and you don't care that I'm a monkey. You don't care that I can't fly."

As Jasper thought about what Charlie said, they continued with their journey, humming the tune of the song. Jasper soon heard new noises up ahead. They were getting closer to the edge of the jungle. He worried about being this far from home as butterflies fluttered about inside his stomach.

CHAPTER NINE

Was it too late to go back home?

He looked at Charlie who seemed so calm. Jasper smiled and hummed as if he didn't have a care in the world.

If Charlie can do this, then darn it, so can I! Jasper thought.

Jasper had to be on guard. He had his brother to think about.

Charlie drew closer to the two brothers. "They're really nice, by the way. They sometimes give me food."

Jasper knew Charlie loved to eat. In fact, every time Jasper saw Charlie, he always had something to eat within his hands. If these new creatures gave Charlie food, how bad could they be? Yet, Jasper knew he needed to be careful.

"Charlie, does your mama know you take food from these creatures? How can it be safe? They don't live in the jungle."

His mama told him to be careful with anything new to him. If he wasn't sure about it, he needed to stay away.

"They leave food out and always watch from a distance," Charlie said. "We will be careful. You know I wouldn't let anything happen to my two best buds."

The trio came upon a clearing with a small pool of running water in the distance. It was perfect, since they were all thirsty. The cool water slid down Jasper's throat, making his tongue jump with joy.

Oh, wow. That felt good!

Looking up, Jasper saw strange creatures moving about. They didn't look like anything he'd ever seen before. They had two legs like himself, but they didn't have any feathers or a beak. They didn't have a tail like Charlie, or long arms to swing from tree to tree.

"Jasper, don't walk too far in front of me," Willie complained.

"I won't."

Turning to Charlie ... *Wait ... Where was Charlie? He was gone!*

Looking around, Jasper saw his friend walking ahead. He had so many questions to ask. Jasper and Willie caught up with Charlie, who was now sitting by a tree.

He and Willie looked in the direction their friend had his eyes on, straight ahead. What they saw in the near distance was like nothing they'd ever seen before.

"What is all that noise?" Jasper asked.

"Those are the creatures I was telling you about. The square buildings are where they live. It's like my tree and your nest."

"How did you discover them?" Jasper asked.

"My family explores for food and new places to live. My mom showed me this place with the condition to be careful and not get too close. One day, they saw me and when they left, some seeds were on the ground."

Charlie drew closer to the jungle's edge. "Come on, guys," he said.

"Jasper, I think I will stay right here. I'll just watch," Willie said.

"Good idea. I won't be long."

Hurrying to catch up, Jasper saw the unknown creatures look up and wave to Charlie and him. They were so big, even bigger than some of the smaller trees in the jungle.

He lowered his voice and whispered, "What are they?"

"They're called humans," Charlie said.

"They're so different from us."

"Yes, but they've been nice to me," Charlie stated.

The two of them watched the humans in the distance.

Jasper was glad he could fly. But Charlie had never steered him wrong. The fact that they remained near the jungle worked for Jasper.

The humans went about their business.

Jasper and Charlie continued to observe them. Time flew by. The two of them took in the scene before them in silence.

Soon, Charlie stretched. He looked at Jasper.

"So, what do you think?" he asked, nodding at the humans.

"Amazing. I thought the jungle was big, but now I know it's bigger than I first thought. Pretty cool, Charlie. Thank you for showing me."

"What are friends for?" he said with a smile. "Time to head back. I told my mom I wouldn't be gone too long. I'm sure she is waiting for me."

Turning around, Jasper and Charlie made their way back into the forest and to Willie, each with different thoughts of this latest exploration running through their heads.

When Jasper and Charlie reached Willie, he said, "I'm so glad you two are back. Were you scared, Jasper?"

"Nay, it wasn't too bad. We kept our distance. Maybe next time you can come with us."

Willie nodded.

"Time to head back before Mama gets worried," Jasper told his brother.

It wouldn't take long for the three of them to get back home, with one swinging through the branches and the other two flying as they kept pace.

Jasper had thought he knew about the whole world from what he could see from his tree. Yet, as he flew along, he realized he'd never imagined that there was so much more out there.

What an incredible place this was!

Jasper had so much to learn. With his family and friends by his side, he was ready to explore this amazing, colorful world. The rainforest was a great place to live. He couldn't wait to see what was out there next.

Dear reader,

We hope you enjoyed reading *A Rainforest Adventure*. Please take a moment to leave a review in Amazon, even if it's a short one. Your opinion is important to us.

The story continues in *Rainforest Friends and Family*.

To read the first chapter for free, head to https://www.nextchapter.pub/books/rainforest-friends-and-family
Discover more books by Sharon C. Williams at https://www.nextchapter.pub/authors/sharon-c-williams

Want to know when one of our books is free or discounted for Kindle? Join the newsletter at http://eepurl.com/bqqB3H

Best regards,

Sharon C. Williams and the Next Chapter Team

To my Amazon parrot, Jasper. Without his personality and love for his humans this book would not have been written. He is my personal Muse.

ACKNOWLEDGMENTS

To my family, who has endured me taking on this project. For bearing with me during the times I was feeling neurotic and downright not likeable as I tried to get the words to come out just right.

To my editor, Nancy, whose tireless effort made my words sparkle and come alive. Her dedication and support has helped me through this endeavor. She has believed in me from day one.

To my sister, Karen, who loaned me two of her daycare kids so they could read my book, and give me their opinions. That, in itself, was invaluable. Her support is truly appreciated.

To my friend, Amy, who took the time to go over the query letter that got my manuscript into the hands of several submission editors.

To the editor, Mike Simpson, who even though he rejected my submission, he filled his letter with so much positivity that I framed it. In that letter, he gave me the three reasons why they didn't pick up Jasper. After revising it according to his advice, the book got picked up by a publisher two submissions later. Even though he will not be publishing this book, he deserves a lot of credit for how far this book has come.

To my friend, Debbie, who believed in me from the very moment she read the first draft of Jasper. According to her, she knew this book was going to be published someday.

To Melanie from Fountain Blue Publishing for believing in Jasper and me. I will always be grateful for all that you ddid for the 1st edition. I got to live my dream. That is priceless. I thank you.

To the numerous people on my Twitter account, Facebook profile page, and my website that have encouraged and lifted me up.

To my writing groups in town, all of which have helped me in one way or another with edits and suggestions.

To Kim, my illustrator, who with her patience and talent worked with me on getting the best possible representation of Jasper to come to life for the 1st edition of this book.

To Miika Hannila who took a chance on me for the 2nd edition of this book and their amazing art department. I am grateful.

The list goes on. I am surrounded by a large group of people who have helped me get to this point in time. Without each and every one of you out there, and those listed above, Jasper, Amazon Parrot: A Rainforest Adventure would not have seen the light of day.

ABOUT THE AUTHOR

Sharon C. Williams is a native of New England raised in Northern Maine. She lives in North Carolina with her husband and son. She is also owned by a flock of birds. Sharon has a B. S. degree in Chemistry. She loves to read, sketch, take pictures, walk, exercise, go to the movies, and listen to music. She is a budding bird watcher, and knits on the side. She is a huge sports fan of baseball, basketball, hockey, and football. She is also a shutterbug and is always looking for the next big shot. Two of her short stories were published in the anthology, *Cassandra's Roadhouse*, which is no longer published. Sharon also has two short stories published in the *Dragons in the Attic* anthology, which was written by her writing group, The Wonder Chicks. Her children's chapter book, *Jasper, Amazon Parrot: A Rainforest Adventure*, and *Jasper: Amazon Friends and Family*, were previously released by Fountain Blue Publishing in 2013 and 2015. Her comedy novel about her war with her backyard squirrels, *Squirrel Mafia*, was also released in the spring of 2015 by Peaceful Musings Publishing, followed by an anthology titled *Everyday Musings,* which was published in in 2016 by Lysestrah Press. She finished 2016 with two short stories in the anthology *The Reading Corner: Book One* which was released by Fountain Blue Publishing.